The Bird House

The Bird House

by CYNTHIA RYLANT

Illustrations by
BARRY MOSER

THE BLUE SKY PRESS

An Imprint of Scholastic Inc. • New York

THE BLUE SKY PRESS

Text copyright © 1998 by Cynthia Rylant
Illustrations copyright © 1998 by Barry Moser
All rights reserved.

The Blue Sky Press is a registered trademark of Scholastic Inc.

Library of Congress catalog card number: 97-25415
ISBN 0-590-47345-X

10 9 8 7 6 5 4 3 2 1   8 9/9 0/0 01 02 03

Printed in Singapore   46
First printing, September 1998

For Cindy Mills Saddler
—C.R.

To the memory of
my friend Roosevelt
—B.M.

ONCE A BRIGHT BLUE house stood beside a river.

Birds loved this house. They were always flying by. Sparrows
sat on windowsills. Swallows slept in the chimney. Wrens flew
in and out. And a great barred owl roosted above the front door.

A young girl who was walking along the river one day saw this house. She was a girl without a home or a family, and she had not been happy for a very long time.

But when she saw all the birds around the bright house, her face lit up, and she stayed, hidden in the trees, to watch.

Presently the front door opened, and an old woman stepped outside. The birds all scattered and flew when the old woman appeared. All except the great barred owl. He never moved.

But the scattering birds quickly came back. Nuthatches ran down the roof. Hummingbirds looked in through the windows. And a sweet cooing dove followed the old woman everywhere she went.

The young girl, hidden in the trees, was amazed.

The next day the birds were back at the bright blue house, and so was the girl. She watched as goldfinches hopped up and down the front steps, purple martins lined up on the eaves, and a large blue heron walked among the sunflowers.

Again, she watched as the old woman stepped outside and the birds scattered. All except the great barred owl. He never moved.

On the third day the girl came yet again to the house, and there were woodpeckers on the mailbox, blue jays on the shutters, and a pheasant on the welcome mat.

And again, as the girl watched, the old woman appeared.

But, surprisingly, the birds did not scatter. This day, instead, they rose as one into the sky. The birds flew first east, then west, north, then south. They flew and formed perfectly a word: GIRL.

The young girl saw this word in the sky, and she ran away as fast as she could. But the old woman stood still, watching the birds and trying to understand what they were telling her.

For many days the young girl was afraid to return to the bright blue house, afraid of being found out by the old woman.

But the girl loved the birds so much that finally she could not stay away. She had to see them again. She returned and hid among the trees.

She saw thrushes on the clothesline, starlings in the wheelbarrow, and cardinals all over the picket fence.

But as soon as the door opened and the old woman stepped
out, the girl jumped up to run away. She did not want the birds
to write anything in the sky again.

This time, however, the birds did not move at all when the old woman appeared. They did not scatter. They did not fly. They did not write anything in the sky. They stayed on the clothesline, in the wheelbarrow, on the picket fence, perfectly still.

Then, one lone bird raised its wings to fly.

The great barred owl, who never moved, suddenly lifted up. He lifted his enormous, silent wings and swiftly, surely, he swooped into the trees. And before she could get away, the young girl was

caught in the owl's talons. He calmly held on to her shirt, until
the old woman—hearing the girl's cries—found them.

The old woman was not really that surprised to see a girl.
She took the child into the bright blue house, and she washed
the dirt from the girl's face and fed her bread and beans. Then
the old woman talked with her, all through the night.

And since that time, the girl has always lived with the old woman. Each day they step outside to tend the flowers or the pumpkins or perhaps just to take a walk. The birds are always there, and, of course, they always scatter when the door opens and the woman and girl appear.

All except one: the great barred owl.

He never moves.

But he always nods his head to the girl whenever she walks past. And the girl always smiles back.

The text for Cynthia Rylant's

The Bird House

was set in Eric Gill's Joanna,

designed in 1930 for Hague & Gill.

It was named after Mr. Gill's daughter, Joanna.

The display type used is Poetica.

The illustrations were executed in transparent watercolor

on May Linen, a paper made by hand and specially sized

for Mr. Moser by Katherine and Howard Clark

at Twinrocker Handmade Papers in Brookston, Indiana.

Production supervision by Jessica Allan

Designed by Barry Moser and Kathleen Westray